W9-CDI-645

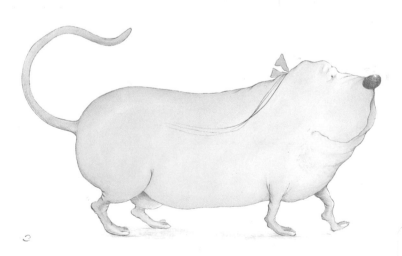

My Sister Gracie

G i l l i a n   J o h n s o n

Tundra Books

Copyright © 2000 by Gillian Johnson

Published in Canada by Tundra Books, *McClelland & Stewart Young Readers*,
481 University Avenue, Toronto, Ontario M5G 2E9

Published in the United States by Tundra Books of Northern New York,
P.O. Box 1030, Plattsburgh, New York 12901

Library of Congress Catalog Number: 00-131207

Canadian Cataloguing in Publication Data

Johnson, Gillian
My sister gracie

ISBN 0-88776-514-9

I. Title.

PS8569.O327M8 2000   jC813'.54   C00-930417-7
PZ7.J65My 2000

We acknowledge the support of the Canada Council for the Arts
and the Ontario Arts Council for our publishing program.

We acknowledge the financial support of the Government of Canada through the
Book Publishing Industry Development Program for our publishing activities.

Book design by Kong Njo

Printed in Hong Kong

1 2 3 4 5 6   05 04 03 02 01 00

For Nicholas

Once upon a time ago
There lived a dog named Fabio.

In many ways he had it all –
A bone to chew, a rubber ball,
A teddy bear, a leafy tree,
A furry rug, a family.

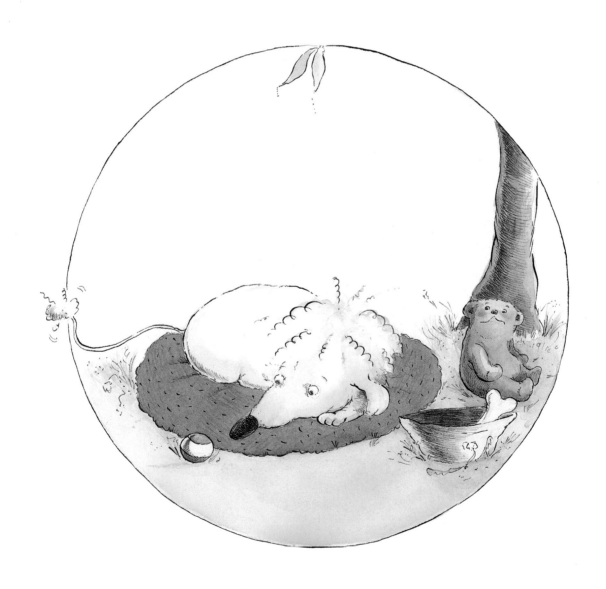

So why did Fabio
Mope and moan
In spite of the ball,
the bear,
the bone?
Why was he sulky,
Sad and snappy?

"A brother would make a sad dog happy."

The family decided the time had come
To have TWO dogs instead of one.
"For a present we'll get you a friend," they said.

That night, as Fabio lay in bed . . .

He dreamed of a baby thoroughbred.

He'd take his brother
To the park.
They'd sniff the world
Till it was dark.

They'd share his bone,
They'd toss the ball,
They'd chew the rug,
They'd do it all.

"I'm getting a brother!
Yes, it's true!"
Now all the dogs in
The neighborhood knew.

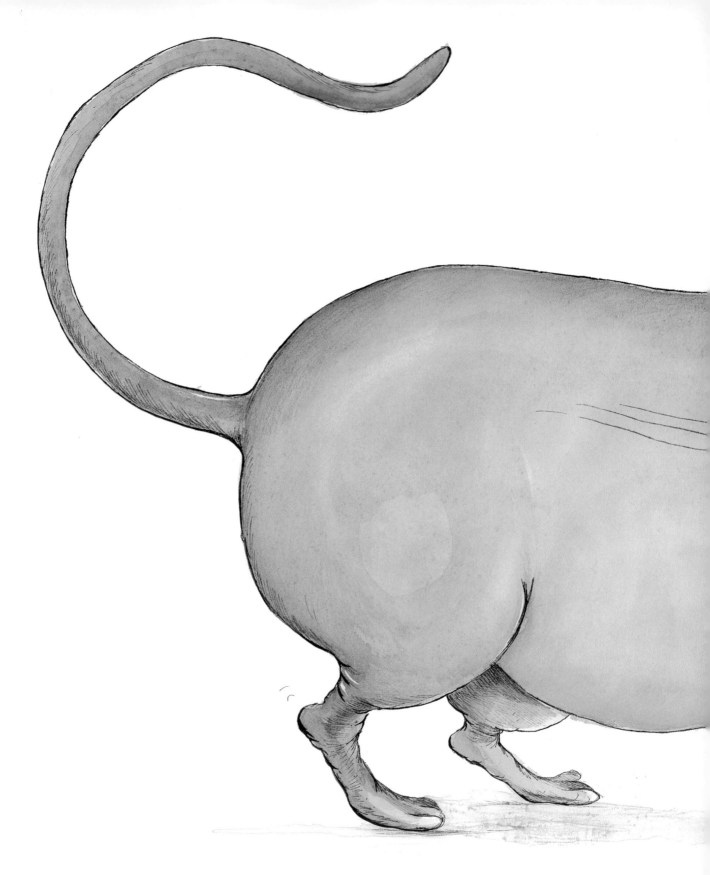

So imagine how Fabio felt when he found

they had brought for his present a GIRL . . . from the pound!

Gracie was large and lacking zest.
They said, "She'll need a lot of rest."

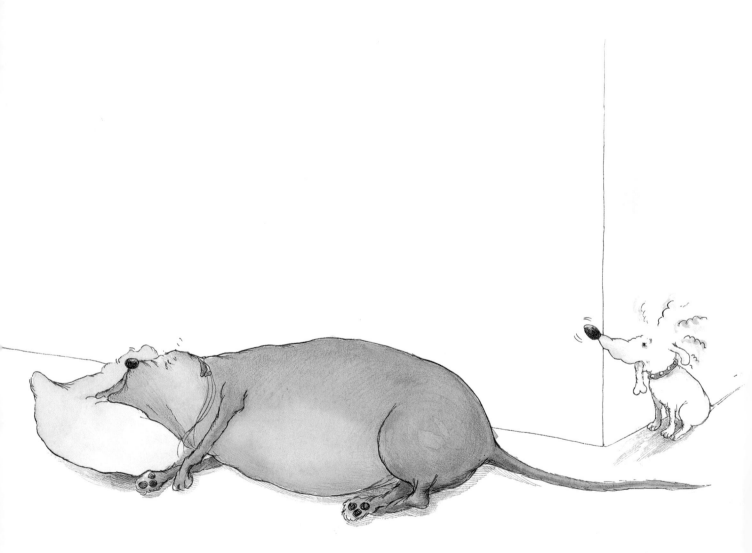

She did not want to tour the park
And sniff the world till it was dark.
She did not want to share his bone.
(At the pound she'd had her own.)
She did not want to
Chase the ball.
(She slipped on it
and took a fall.)
She did not want to
Chew the rug.

All she wanted was a hug.

"I'd rather have a *parakeet*
Than a hound that sleeps and overeats."

"Forget him, Gracie, he's a grouch.
Come and join us on the couch."

When Fabio tried to share the fun
They pushed him down . . .

What HAD he done?

Now why is Fabio sad and snappy?
Gracie was meant to make him happy.
Why do his tears fall down like rain?
"If Gracie would go, I'd laugh again."

"Gracie," they said, "has come to stay.
She isn't going to go away."

So Fabio made a little plan –
And acting like a gentleman
He said to Gracie,
"Come with me.
We'll take a walk and it will be
A lot of fun for you, you'll see."

"Just wait ten steps and follow me."
(He did not want his friends to see.)

"Well, good-bye, Gracie.
You were nice to know.
But now it's time for you to
Go."

"Didn't you hear me?"
Fabio frowned.
"I told you – walk yourself back
To the pound!"

A sudden rustle.
A "Hey!"
And a "Ho!"
Nowhere to hide!
Nowhere to go!

They circled round him,
Said, "Hello,
Where's your BROTHER,
Fabio?"

Out popped Gracie, smiling wide.
"What's your BROTHER'S name?" they cried.

They laughed and teased.
They sniggered, "Your brother?
She's old enough to be your mother!"

The littlest stood
On tippy toes.
She scrunched her eyes
And wrinkled her nose.

"Hey, Fatso, you're an
Ugly hound.
Were you the last one at
The pound?"

Fabio bristled.
The reason why?
He saw a tear
In Gracie's eye.
That little dog
Just one-foot high
Had made his sister,
Gracie, cry!

Fabio growled.
He shook his head.
"We've had enough
Of this," he said.

"She may not chew
My bone or ball,
But she's my sister
After all."

"Yes, Gracie's my sister,
It's really true.
Now excuse us –
We have a *rendezvous*."

Then brother and sister
Went off to the park
And sniffed the world
Till it was dark.